A Junior Novelization

Based on the original screenplay by Elise Allen
Adapted by Nicole Corse
Illustrations by Ulkutay Design Group

D0354721

SCHOLASTIC INC.

New York   Toronto   London   Auckland

Sydney   Mexico City   New Delhi   Hong Kong

ISBN 978-0-545-22864-0

Copyright © 2011 Mattel, Inc. All rights reserved. BARBIE and associated trademarks and trade dress are owned by, and used under license from, Mattel, Inc.

Published by Scholastic Inc. SCHOLASTIC and associated logos are trademarks and/or registered trademarks of Scholastic Inc.

12 11 10 9 8 7 6 5 4 3 2 1   11 12 13 14 15 16/0

Printed in the U.S.A.   40

First printing, March 2011

Designed by Angela Jun

Special thanks to Vicki Jaeger, Monica Okazaki, Kathleen Warner, Emily Kelly, Sarah Quesenberry, Julia Phelps, Tanya Mann, Rob Hudnut, Tiffany J. Shuttleworth, M. Elizabeth Hughes, Carla Alford, Angus Cameron, Tulin Ulkutay, Ayse Ulkutay, and Walter Martishuis

Chapter 1

It was the night of the premiere of Barbie's newest movie, and she was so excited! She had spent all afternoon getting ready with the help of her super-fab stylists, Taylor and Carrie. Taylor knew everything about clothes, especially shoes. She had picked out a gorgeous, sparkling gown for Barbie's red carpet premiere. Carrie's specialty was handbags and accessories. Purses came first, but she was also an expert with scarves, hats, sunglasses, jewelry, gloves, and even feathered boas. Barbie felt so beautiful wearing their newest masterpiece. She was so lucky to have such amazing stylists!

Barbie walked outside and got into a black super-stretch limo with her boyfriend, Ken. As they were driving to the premiere, Barbie thought about how much fun it would be to see all her fans and share this special night with them.

On the red carpet, Carrie and Taylor were already being interviewed by a reporter named Tracey. Tracey turned to the camera. "Tracey Clinger here, at the premiere of Barbie's latest movie, where top stylists Taylor and Carrie are sharing their secrets for dressing a superstar. Taylor, what's it like?"

"I can sum it up in one word, Tracey—" Taylor started.

"Taylor! Look, it's Crystal! It's really her! Let's say hi—it's been forever!" Carrie said as she began pulling Taylor over to their friend.

"Wait! What about the one word?" Tracey shouted as they disappeared into the crowd.

"That one word is . . . Raquelle," said a girl who suddenly appeared next to Tracey. It was Barbie's costar, Raquelle.

"Raquelle, hello! I'm here with the one and only Raquelle. We're so thrilled you could make it!" Tracey smiled to the camera.

"Oh, I wouldn't miss it, Tracey. It gives me a chance to keep in touch with all my adoring fans," Raquelle replied as she yanked an autograph book and pen out of a little girl's hands.

"Hey! That's for Barbie!" the little girl

3

exclaimed as she grabbed her book back. Raquelle gave her a mean look.

"You know, Tracey," Raquelle continued, "the best part of this movie was working with—"

"Barbie!" shouted Tracey as she spotted Barbie across the way. She raced toward her, almost knocking Raquelle over.

"I did not say 'Barbie!'" Raquelle shouted after Tracey. "'A great script' is what I was going to say." She turned to the cameraman. "You can edit that so I come out looking good, right?" she asked.

The black super-stretch limo pulled up right in front of the red carpet. As soon as the car door opened, Barbie was almost blinded by all of the camera flashes that were going off! Stepping out of the car and onto the red carpet, Barbie and Ken posed for some glamorous pictures.

Tracey couldn't wait to interview Barbie. "What star quality! And that dress is gorgeous on you! Can you take a few steps so we can see it in action?" Tracey thought Barbie's dress was beautiful. It would certainly get rave reviews by all the top fashion magazines.

Barbie was flattered. "Of course! Carrie and Taylor are geniuses." She glowed as she began to turn.

Nearby, Raquelle was listening to Barbie's interview. She had had enough of Barbie always being in the spotlight. While Barbie twirled to show Tracey her dress, Raquelle saw her chance. She walked behind Barbie and stepped on her dress's train — causing it to tear all the way up the back!

"Oh, no!" Barbie gasped as she turned bright red. She turned around and saw Raquelle grinning behind her. Barbie could not believe that Raquelle had ruined her dress on purpose!

Luckily, Tracey did not notice that Barbie's dress had been torn. She continued the interview. "I love your dress! It's so light and breezy," she said.

Carrie and Taylor saw the whole thing happen, and they immediately rushed over to help. Carrie quickly stood behind Barbie so that no one would be able to see the rip. Taylor walked up next to Barbie. "Barbie, you promised you'd come to me for a touch-up before going on camera!" Taylor said to give Barbie an excuse to leave the interview.

Barbie turned to Tracey. "It looks like I have to be going. Thank you for your time!" she called as she briskly walked away with Carrie following close behind to cover up the rip.

Barbie turned to Taylor and Carrie once they were away from the cameras. "I can't believe Raquelle purposely ripped my dress!" Barbie said as Taylor examined the large tear behind her. Taylor knew the rip

was too large to fix unless she used a little magic. Barbie didn't know it, but Taylor and Carrie were actually fairies in disguise! While Barbie wasn't looking, Taylor did her magical Z-snap. The dress glowed with sparkles and was instantly repaired!

"No worries," Taylor said. "Good as new."

"What? What do you mean?" asked Barbie. But as Barbie turned to see, she no longer needed an answer. Carrie was holding the train of her dress and it no longer had a rip in it! Before Barbie could figure out how the dress was repaired, Ken came over.

"Everyone's heading in for the movie premiere. Is everything okay?" he asked.

"Everything's great," Barbie said as she turned to Carrie and Taylor. "I don't know how you did it, but I totally owe you. You two are lifesavers! Lunch at Wally's tomorrow?"

"Sold like half-price glitter flats!" Carrie said.

"Now go see your movie!" Taylor added with a smile.

Barbie was really happy that her dress was no longer ruined. She was so thankful to have such amazing and talented friends like Carrie and Taylor. Linking her arm with Ken's, Barbie walked into the theater.

Carrie and Taylor turned to each other and shared their secret fairy handshake—complete with glittery magic sparkles. All of a sudden, they noticed someone was behind them.

"I saw that!" a voice called.

Carrie and Taylor gasped. But when they turned around they found out it was only Crystal, their old friend. Crystal was very beautiful and dressed to perfection. She also wore a very glittery camera that looked like a pendant around her neck. Carrie had seen her taking pictures with it all night.

"Crystal! Sit with us in the movie!" Carrie said. Crystal shook her head. There was important business she had to attend to. "I have to go back. Fashion pictures for Princess Graciella, you see. Enjoy the movie!" Crystal walked away. Carrie and Taylor headed into the theater.

"So what do you think, Princess Graciella?" Crystal asked as she leaned over a beautiful fairy to whom she was showing her pictures from the premiere.

"Crystal, it's just a human movie premiere. Can't this wait?" Crystal did not respond. She simply set a colorful goblet down next to the princess. As Princess Graciella took a sip from the goblet, Crystal smiled.

Crystal pressed the button on her camera necklace and the room flashed. Suddenly, a picture of Ken at the premiere appeared. "Wait! Who is that?" asked Princess Graciella. "He's beautiful!"

"Um, I don't know. Just someone at the premiere, I guess . . ." Crystal trailed off.

Princess Graciella's eyes flashed. "I'm . . . I'm in love with him. I must have him!"

"Completely understandable," Crystal responded. "Consider him all yours. . . ."

Chapter 2

The day after the premiere, Barbie joined Ken, Taylor, and Carrie for some ice cream sundaes at their favorite spot, Wally's Diner. Barbie could see Raquelle sitting in another booth across the restaurant. She thought about confronting her about last night, but she just wanted to enjoy being with her friends.

"Barbie, last night's movie was incredible! You and comedy are like a miniskirt and knee-high boots: perfect together!" Taylor said. Barbie turned to thank Taylor for her compliment, as Raquelle walked over to their table.

"Hey, Barbie!" Raquelle said. "Fun time last night! Great to see you ripping things up!" As Raquelle turned to leave, she sent one last glance back at Ken. She put her hand up near her ear and said, "Call me." Then she smiled and walked outside. Barbie was furious!

Barbie had had enough. "That is it!" she said as she stood up to follow Raquelle.

"Where are you going?" Ken asked.

"I have to stick up for myself. What she did last night is *so* not okay, and I am going to call her on it!" Barbie headed for Raquelle. Ken, Taylor, and Carrie followed.

"Raquelle," she called out as she walked outside. "We need to talk!"

"Whatever about?" Raquelle innocently replied.

Before Barbie could answer, a strange voice cried, "There he is, Princess!" Barbie looked around to see where the voice came from. There were three fairies flying toward them! She turned to her friends to make sure she wasn't imagining things. No one could believe what they were seeing!

"He's perfect! We're going to get married! Girls, bring him back to the palace!" Princess Graciella ordered. Suddenly, two fairies swooped down and grabbed Ken, lifting him off into the sky. It happened so quickly that no one could stop them.

"KEN!" Barbie cried. "Let him go!"

"Let me down! Hey! What's going on?" Ken yelled as he flailed his legs.

"You heard her—a wedding! Isn't that beautiful?" Crystal replied.

Barbie was completely shocked, but she could not prepare herself for what happened next. All of a sudden, Taylor and Carrie spread their own wings and flew after the other fairies!

Barbie turned to Raquelle. "I am not seeing this. Are you seeing this?"

"Only if you're seeing it. You're not seeing it, right?" Raquelle replied as she pinched herself to make sure she wasn't dreaming.

"*So* not seeing it," said Barbie, trying to convince herself. But then she looked toward the sky and saw Ken flying farther away. "Ken!" she cried helplessly as she watched Carrie and Taylor trying to catch up to him.

"Stay away! You do not get to spoil my wedding day!" Princess Graciella yelled back to Carrie and Taylor. And then in an instant, she, Ken, and the other fairies vanished. They had flown through a wing-shaped, glittery opening in the sky that quickly closed behind them. Carrie and Taylor hadn't made it in time.

Carrie and Taylor flew back to the

ground, quickly hiding their wings.

"You. How? You flew!" Barbie said with amazement.

"What are you?" asked Raquelle.

"Umm . . . I don't know what you're talking about. It must have been a trick of the light," Carrie said unconvincingly.

"A trick of the light?! You just busted out wings and flew! How can that be a trick of the light?" Raquelle demanded.

"Umm . . . it can't . . . but that's what the fairy handbook says we're supposed to say if we're caught," Carrie replied.

"The fairy handbook? What's that?" Barbie asked.

"A handbook for fairies. . . . I mean—" Carrie turned to Taylor. "Taylor, this isn't going very well," she whispered.

"Carrie, forget it. We can't give them an

excuse after what they saw," Taylor said. "It's time you learned the fairy secret: Carrie and I are fairies. So are those other girls."

Barbie and Raquelle were not buying it. "Okay," Raquelle said. "Except there's no such thing as fairies."

"Of course there is," Taylor explained. "And you see us all the time—you don't realize it 'cause we keep our wings hidden. We come from Gloss Angeles, and—"

"Whoa, whoa, whoa—*Gloss* Angeles?" Barbie interrupted. "I so get this now! We're being pranked. The studio must have set this up to promote our new movie. Can we do another take? I'll give you way more with another take," she said as she fixed her hair.

Taylor realized she needed to be a lot

more convincing. "This isn't a stunt!" she said. "We're real fairies! I'm a Shoe Fairy, Carrie's a Purse Fairy, and Ken's in real danger!"

Barbie was worried. "What kind of danger?" she asked, hoping for the best.

"Humans can visit Gloss Angeles," Taylor explained, "but Princess Graciella said she was marrying Ken. If a human comes to Gloss Angeles and marries a fairy, that human has to stay in Gloss Angeles . . . forever."

"It's fairy law," Carrie said solemnly.

Barbie could not believe what she was hearing. "We have to save him! We have to get him back!"

Raquelle looked at Taylor. "So if you're real, then Ken really is in trouble. How do we save him?" she asked.

"We?" Barbie asked with surprise.

"Yeah, we! He's my friend, too. So, how do we save him?" Raquelle asked Carrie and Taylor.

Taylor held up her magical phone. She turned to Barbie and Raquelle, showing them the picture. "We go shopping. . . ."

Chapter 3

Meanwhile, Ken was facing a very confusing situation of his own. He knew he was in a large palace. He also knew he was being held prisoner by some very sparkly kidnappers. Other than that, he really had no idea what was going on. He started to feel queasy.

"Okay, first couple picture. Get together and say 'fair-ies,'" Crystal said, so that Ken and Princess Graciella would smile at the camera. The princess was beaming with joy, but the confused look on Ken's face was far from a smile. Crystal snapped the picture with her camera necklace. "Love it!"

"Let go of me!" Ken yelled to the fairies holding him in the air.

"As you wish, darling," Princess Graciella said, nodding to her attendants. They released Ken, but he began to fall. "Gentle with my fiancé!" Princess Graciella ordered, and the attendants rushed to catch him.

"Your what?" Ken exclaimed. "No. Look, I don't know who you are or what you are, but you've made a mistake. I'm not marrying anyone! I'm—"

Ken was suddenly interrupted by the door opening. In walked a very handsome male fairy. Crystal seemed especially excited to see him.

"Zane!" she exclaimed as she twisted her

hair flirtatiously. "So, how are things?" But Zane pushed right past her, heading straight for Ken.

"You! You THIEF!" he yelled at Ken. "Is it true what I hear? You plan to steal my love, Princess Graciella?"

"No!" Ken started to explain.

"Yes!" cried Princess Graciella. "I'm going to marry . . ." She turned to Ken. "What's your name, sweetie?" she asked.

"Ken," Ken answered, defeated.

"Ben!" Princess Graciella turned to Zane. "Ben is the love of my life, and we're marrying at sundown!" She grabbed Ken's arm and wrapped it around her shoulders. Ken pulled his arm away, but not before Zane noticed.

"No! Wait," Ken protested. "I'm in love with someone else."

"Kevin!" Princess Graciella gasped. "How could you say such a thing? And on our wedding day!" she sobbed, bursting into tears.

"Oh, come on. Don't cry. . . . My name is Ken, and . . . look, I don't even know you!" Ken tried to calm her.

Zane had had enough. "I challenge you to a duel! We will fight to see who's more worthy of Princess Graciella's love," he said as he gave Ken an intimidating look.

Princess Graciella couldn't wait for the duel. "Attendants," she ordered, "gather the weapons and help them prepare!"

"I'll help you, Zane!" Crystal said with excitement.

"Good-bye, my darling. I'll see you at the duel," Princess Graciella said to Ken.

"You're leaving me here with him?" Ken cried.

"Oh, don't worry. He won't hurt you," Princess Graciella assured him. "Well, not until the duel." She kissed Ken on the cheek and flew out the door. She was gone.

"Wait!" Ken cried as he raced after her. "Let me out of here!" he yelled as he pounded on the closed door. Ken was trapped.

Chapter 4

"Raquelle, come on! Carrie said just to grab something so we blend in. We're not actually trying things on," Barbie said.

Raquelle could barely see over the pile of clothes she had in her arms. "I know, but they all look so cute. I bet Ken would flip for me in this purple one. What do you think?" she asked. Barbie gave her a look. "What?" Raquelle asked innocently.

Taylor and Carrie were walking over to them with a dressing room attendant.

"Your best fitting room, please," Taylor

said as she gently moved her hand and sparkles sprinkled into the air.

The dressing room attendant saw the sparkles and looked at Taylor with a knowing smile. "Right this way," she said. She walked them over to a locked fitting room all the way in the back. Clothes were hanging over the door. "You'll want this one." The dressing room attendant smiled.

"But this one looks like it's being used," Barbie pointed out politely.

Carrie giggled. "Doesn't it? Haven't you noticed there's one stall in every fitting room that's always closed, even though no one's ever in it?"

"Yes! That's a fairy thing?" Barbie realized.

"Right!" Carrie said excitedly. "We call it a fairy flyway!"

Things were starting to make sense to Barbie. "So that means . . . the fitting room attendant is . . ."

"Yes, a fairy!" Taylor said. Barbie looked back at the attendant. As the attendant waved good-bye, sparkles fell from her fingers. Barbie smiled.

Once everyone was inside the room, the door shut behind them. As soon as it closed, Barbie could see a bright white flash. She closed her eyes, not knowing what to expect next.

Barbie opened her eyes. She could see the entire city of Paris beneath her. There was only one place in Paris with such a spectacular view—the Eiffel Tower! "Are we really in Paris? But how?" Barbie asked.

"The fairy flyway—flyways are fairy

shortcuts to spots all over the globe. We had to come to Paris. It's home to the one Gloss Angeles portal Princess Graciella couldn't lock—the personal portal of Lilianna Roxelle," explained Taylor.

"Lilianna Roxelle, the famous fashion editor?" Barbie asked.

"She's also the oldest and wisest fairy living in the human world. She has a portal that even Princess Graciella can't close," Carrie explained.

"Want to see her?" Taylor asked.

"Sure," Barbie replied. "But how are we going to get down?"

Taylor held out her hand to Barbie.

Raquelle saw that Carrie was holding out her hand to her as well. "No. Oh, no. No way. I have a strict rule: no plane, no fly," Raquelle said nervously.

"You'll love it. Honestly!" Carrie encouraged her.

Barbie felt nervous. "You're sure you can do this?" she asked Taylor.

"I'm a Shoe Fairy," Taylor explained. "The more fabulous my shoes, the stronger my magic. Check out these babies." She stuck out her foot and showed off her amazing shoe.

Barbie and Raquelle were impressed. "If I had to trust my life to one pair of shoes, it would be those," Raquelle admitted.

Barbie and Raquelle looked at each other. They had to face what was to come if they were going to rescue Ken. The four leaped off the Eiffel Tower. Carrie and Taylor spread their wings and suddenly they were all flying!

The lights of Paris twinkled under the flying foursome as they soared above landmarks like the Arc de Triomphe and Notre Dame. They descended toward an elegant building ringed by balconies.

"This is Liliana's apartment," Taylor said as they landed on a balcony.

Barbie knocked on the sliding glass door. "Ms. Roxelle?"

"Ah, hello, fairy friend," a voice called as the door opened.

"Hi, Ms. Roxelle," Taylor and Carrie said together as they greeted her with a special fairy handshake.

"Carrie and Taylor, right? What brings you here?"

"Ms. Roxelle, we have a problem, and Carrie and Taylor thought you could help," Barbie explained.

"Perhaps I can. Please, come in!"

A few minutes later Barbie was having tea with the rest of her friends in Lilianna's fairy sitting room. All of the furniture magically rose high into the glass dome of her beautiful atrium, with room for fairy wings. Barbie had been explaining to Lilianna what brought them to her doorstep.

"So Princess Graciella flew off with Ken and said she'd marry him?" asked Lilianna.

"Then closed all the portals. Except yours, of course," Taylor continued.

"Of course. And I'll let you use it. But you might need something more. Did you notice the color of Princess Graciella's eyes?" Lilianna asked.

"Yes! They were violet! The perfect

match to a sweet pair of boots I bought last week," replied Taylor.

But that didn't make sense to Carrie. "But Princess Graciella has blue eyes."

"Then she has taken a love potion," explained Lilianna. "The potion adds a little red, the color of love, to the eyes. The red turns blue eyes purple, and that's how you can tell."

Lilianna leaped off her seat and flew to a cabinet. "Not much left, but enough for one dose," she said as she handed a near-empty vial to Barbie. "Here. Release this

mist directly above Princess Graciella so it can rain down on her. That will break the potion's spell."

"Thanks," Barbie said, eager to help Ken.

"Let's go!" Raquelle agreed.

"Now come; I'll take you to my portal." Carrie and Taylor helped Barbie and Raquelle down from their chairs. They followed Lilianna down the hallway and through the foyer. Then Lilianna turned to Carrie and Taylor, realizing something.

"Oh, no. You're not going with them, are you? I thought you were banned from Gloss Angeles," Lilianna said to Carrie and Taylor.

"You know?" Carrie asked, surprised.

"You are? Why?" Raquelle asked.

"It's a long story," Taylor explained. "But we're going back anyway."

"But you face years in the dungeons if you're caught!" Lilianna warned.

Carrie nodded. "Friends stick together, especially when things are rough."

"Exactly," Taylor agreed. "Barbie has always helped us, so we're going to help her . . . and Raquelle." She paused and turned to face Lilianna. "Is it still okay if we use your portal?" she asked.

"But of course," Lilianna replied with a smile.

"Bye, Liliana! Thank you!" Barbie called as the group headed to the portal.

"We really appreciate it," Raquelle added.

"Bye-bye! And good luck!" Lilianna said as she watched the friends disappear into the magic portal.

Chapter 5

The girls emerged from the magic portal. Barbie and Raquelle looked around. They could see a gorgeous sparkling city in front of them full of beautiful buildings and amazing fairies! It was truly an awesome sight.

"It's incredible. I can't believe it's real," Barbie said in amazement.

Raquelle looked down. "I can't believe it's so high in the air. How far down is the ground?"

"Ground?" Carrie asked.

"Yeah, the ground! I mean, if I fell,

sooner or later I'd hit the . . ." She could see Carrie and Taylor shaking their heads. "Oh. There's . . . no . . . ground," she realized.

"That's okay," Barbie tried to reassure her. "We'll just hold on to Carrie and Taylor, like before."

"On a rescue mission?" Taylor asked, shaking her head. "Too risky. If there's trouble you might have to fly on your own."

"We can't fly on our own!" Raquelle exclaimed.

"Yet," Taylor added, turning to Carrie.

Carrie knew what Taylor meant. She turned to the girls and exclaimed, "Oh, goody! We get to go to Wings and Things!"

Usually Barbie loved shopping but this trip was taking a sour turn. The shop attendant told Barbie that Ken and the princess were going to be married at sunset.

Barbie couldn't believe that she only had until sunset to save him!

There was no time to lose. They stepped out of the shop and started to flap their new clip-on wings. Barbie felt a rush of excitement as she flew a foot in the air. Then she tried it again and went two feet in the air. She laughed with amazement. "Look at this! I'm flying . . . sort of."

"Think you can try it for real?" asked Taylor.

Raquelle turned to Barbie. "I'll do it if you do it."

"Flying is all about riding the wind currents," Carrie explained. "Come on!"

Barbie encouraged Raquelle, taking her hand. The two girls leaped up. Once they felt balanced, they released each other's hands and surfed the wind currents. Barbie was so excited. "Yes! We're rockin' it, Raquelle!"

But Raquelle ignored Barbie. She turned to fly over to Carrie and Taylor. "So, now we have wings. How do we find Ken?" she asked them.

"I'm sure Princess Graciella took him to the palace. It's the highest point in Gloss Angeles," Taylor said as she pointed up. Barbie and Raquelle looked up and saw a shiny dot in the distance.

Back at the palace, Ken was preparing for his duel as best he could. He was standing with Princess Graciella's attendants, and on the other side of the room Zane was talking with Crystal. Princess Graciella was hovering in the air above them.

"Duelists, stand before me and face each other!" she ordered. "Deploy your wings!"

At that moment, Zane spread out his enormous wings. They were really strong and large. Ken took a deep breath. Poof! He spread out a very small pair of clip-on wings.

Princess Graciella turned to her attendants. "Really?" she asked.

"It was the only clip-on pair we had," one of the fairies explained.

"Oh, whatever. Go to your corners and prepare, gentlemen! I'll be back before the wedding. May the best man win." She turned to Ken. "That means you," she whispered in his ear.

Graciella turned to leave, and Zane glared threateningly at Ken. *How am I going to get out of this one?* Ken wondered.

Chapter 6

The sun was setting lower by the second, and Barbie was hoping she wasn't too late to save Ken! She couldn't imagine him staying in Gloss Angeles forever! Carrie and Taylor were flying in front of her and Raquelle.

"Watch your flight! Turbulence!" Taylor cried out.

Barbie felt the sudden gust of wind. Taylor and Carrie seemed to manage it ahead, but suddenly Raquelle lost her balance. She grabbed on to Barbie. Barbie, too, lost her balance and began tumbling in the air.

"Whooaaa!" they both cried. But then something swooped up under Barbie. She looked down. It was an adorable pony with wings. Barbie couldn't help smiling at the beautiful creature. Raquelle was riding on one next to her. There were several other ponies all in different colors flying around them.

"Aww! You found the pegaponies!" said Carrie.

"Amazing! They're known for being extremely shy. They only come out around people they like," explained Taylor.

"Really?" asked Raquelle. "Thank you. I'm honored," she said as she petted her new friend.

"Me too," Barbie echoed.

Raquelle had an idea. "Maybe we could ride on the pegaponies to the palace."

"Oh, I'd love to! Let's do it!" Carrie said as she turned to the ponies. "That is, if any of you would be willing to give Taylor and me a ride."

A pony flew under her, and another picked up Taylor. They all flew off with renewed hope in their hearts.

The friends kept flying higher and higher. After a while, Barbie could see the palace taking shape ahead.

"There's the palace! Let's go!" Barbie shouted.

"Wait—" said Taylor, but Barbie had already taken off and couldn't hear her. Suddenly, Barbie's pegapony reared back and stopped completely.

"What happened?" Barbie asked, lightly petting her pony's mane. "Are you okay?"

"They won't go any farther because of those," Taylor explained as she pointed up. Everyone looked up. They saw a wide range of random tornadolike wind currents.

"Those are swirlnados: incredibly treacherous wind currents used to protect the palace. Even the most expert flyer will lose her balance and fall if she gets caught in one," Taylor said.

Barbie had an idea. "Raquelle can do it," she said with confidence.

"She can?" Taylor and Carrie asked.

"I can?" Raquelle echoed in disbelief.

"You can," Barbie said without a hint of doubt in her voice. "No one handles horses like you. If anyone can lead us through the swirlnados, it's you."

"How do you know I'm good with horses?" Raquelle asked.

"Are you kidding? We were in riding camp together the summer after tenth grade. You were incredible," Barbie said.

Raquelle was shocked. "I didn't think you even noticed I was there."

"How could I not notice? You were the best rider there! You're brilliant at it, and horses trust you. If you lead the way, I know we can make it to the palace in time to save Ken."

"Okay. Let's do it, but stay close. I want your three pegaponies right behind mine." Raquelle leaned down to her pony. "Don't be scared," she whispered. "I promise we can get through this safely. We just need to work together. Okay, little guy?" she asked. The pegapony immediately calmed down. Raquelle narrowed her eyes and looked up at the swirlnados to decide when to lead her friends into them.

"Now!" she cried.

It seemed as though Raquelle could predict where the swirlnados would appear. Although there were a few close calls, soon Raquelle had successfully led her friends past the last group of swirlnados. They landed their pegaponies and dismounted right next to the palace.

"You did it!" Barbie cheered. She threw her arms around Raquelle, giving her a huge hug.

"Thanks. And thanks for believing I could." Raquelle smiled. "And thank you, pegaponies."

"So, now we just need to get into the palace and find Ken, right?" Barbie asked.

"Exactly," replied Taylor. "But if the palace fairies recognize us, they'll turn us in. So we need a good disguise."

"I'm on it," Carrie said as she reached into her bag. She started pulling out all different kinds of accessories.

"I hope you don't mind me asking, but why were you banned?" asked Barbie.

"We actually don't know why. We used to be friends with Princess Graciella. Then out of nowhere she proclaimed we betrayed her, and according to fairy law that means we are banned," Carrie explained.

"Which is fine," said Taylor. "If that's the way she wants it to be, she can keep Gloss Angeles. Once we save Ken, we'll stay in the human world for good."

Taylor and Carrie put on their disguises. Beneath their new wigs, big sunglasses, and wide hats, they were barely recognizable. "How do we look?" asked Taylor.

"Perfect," said Barbie. "Let's go!"

Chapter 7

Once Barbie and her friends were inside the palace, they heard a shout. It sounded just like Ken!

They raced toward the sound, only to walk right into the middle of a duel! Barbie recognized Princess Graciella watching from above. Barbie looked around the room.

Her heart skipped a beat. There was Ken! He was all right. She also could see another fairy wearing glistening armor. They both had wings, only Ken's were really tiny.

The fairy dueling Ken was soaring high in the air. "What are you doing? Come up here and fight like a fairy!" Zane challenged Ken.

"Stop!" yelled Barbie. She couldn't take it anymore. Ken could not have been happier to see her.

"Barbie! And you've got wings, too?" he said.

"Who dares interrupt my royal duel?" asked Princess Graciella angrily.

Barbie spread her clip-on wings and leaped into the air. She pulled out the magic potion Lilianna gave her to stop the love spell Princess Graciella was under. She was just about to release the mist when Princess Graciella shot a large amount of sparkles in front of her.

"Freeze!" she shouted as the sparkles

spread over Barbie, Raquelle, Carrie, and Taylor.

"I can't move!" Barbie cried.

"None of us can!" said Carrie.

Ken looked at Princess Graciella. "What did you do to them?" he asked accusingly. He turned to Barbie. "Barbie, are you okay?" Ken started to move toward her.

"Don't touch her!" shouted Princess Graciella. "She's nothing to you! You're marrying me, Kyle."

"It's Ken! You don't even know my name! Why would we get married?"

"Because she's under a love potion!" Barbie explained. Looking to the princess, she continued, "Look in the mirror! Your eyes aren't blue anymore. They're violet! That's the sign of the potion!"

"What? That's crazy talk!" Crystal said

a little too quickly. It was obvious she was trying to cover something up.

Zane looked into Princess Graciella's eyes. "You're under a love potion! It all makes sense!"

"You don't realize what you're doing. Let me help. Unfreeze me and I'll remove the spell," Barbie explained.

"Don't listen to her, Princess. She just wants to steal your fiancé," Crystal said.

Zane couldn't believe what he was hearing. "Why are you encouraging this?" he asked Crystal.

But it all was becoming clear to Taylor. "Because she's in love with you! That's why she wants Princess Graciella to marry someone else . . . and why she gave Princess Graciella the love potion."

Princess Graciella was actually starting

to believe this story. "Crystal, is that true?"

Everyone was looking at Crystal. She glanced down, unsure of what to do. And then she spotted them: the shoes. It was her best chance. "Uh, er, those shoes. I know those shoes! Princess Graciella, those fairies are actually Taylor and Carrie!"

Taylor and Carrie were totally caught!

Princess Graciella was going to get to the bottom of this. "Attendants!" she called. Her attendants soared over to Carrie and Taylor, ripping off their disguises. "It is you! And you're still trying to betray me. This time by ruining my wedding!"

"And spreading lies about me!" Crystal added, smiling deviously.

"No, Princess Graciella—" Carrie began.

Princess Graciella decided to banish these fairies once and for all! "Enough!

You're liars—you and your friends!"

She flung out her arms and sent sparkles shooting from each of her hands. Suddenly, Carrie, Taylor, Raquelle, and Barbie were trapped in a pair of magical cages!

"Barbie! Raquelle!" Ken shouted. He turned to Princess Graciella. "What did you do to them?"

"I put them in FurySpheres. The walls are made of pure anger, impervious to force!" she explained.

"Let them go! I'll marry you if I have to, just let them go!" Ken said, feeling helpless.

"You'll marry me either way," Princess Graciella threatened. She shot out a stream of sparkles toward Ken that wrapped around his body. Ken no longer had control of his body! Princess Graciella made him walk toward her. Then she forced him to get down on one knee.

"Princess Graciella, would you do me the honor of being my bride?" Ken asked. Ken gasped in horror. He smacked his hand over his mouth. "That wasn't me! I didn't say that!"

"But you did, my love," replied Princess Graciella. "And I will be your bride. The duel is off!

"Kirby and I have a wedding to attend right now," the princess said as she turned

to Barbie. "I wish you could join us, but you and your friends have an appointment in the dungeons." She waved her hand and the cages flew out of the room.

Ken watched with horror as Barbie flew farther and farther from him. "No! Barbie!" he shouted. But it was too late.

Princess Graciella turned to him, smiling. "Shall we?" she asked as she forced him to lock his arm into hers.

Crystal was also smiling. She turned to Zane. "Girls can be so fickle, can't they?" she said. All Zane could do was look at her with frustration.

Chapter 8

Barbie felt defeated. By now, Ken was probably saying his vows. "It's over. I can't believe we failed," she said.

"No, you did everything you possibly could. We all did," Raquelle reassured her.

"But it wasn't good enough. Now we're caught in a dungeon, and even if we do get out one day, Ken will be married and stuck in Gloss Angeles . . . forever." Barbie started to cry. Everyone was silent. Then Raquelle started to giggle.

"Are you really laughing right now?"

Barbie asked through her tears.

"I'm sorry," said Raquelle. "It's just that if you'd told me yesterday that we'd be stuck in a tiny cage together for who knows how long, I'd have sworn we would have both gone crazy. But now I'm not happy we're stuck, but the being with you part . . . I actually don't mind it."

Barbie smiled. "I'd have said the same thing, but now if I have to be stuck in a tiny cage with someone, I'm actually glad it's you." She paused for a moment. "Why has it always been so bad between us? I feel like from the minute we met, you've always had it in for me."

"Are you kidding? It's the total opposite! The minute we met, you decided I wasn't good enough for you," replied Raquelle.

"I didn't even know you! You wouldn't

say two words to me!" said Barbie.

"Because I was shy!" Raquelle said a little louder than she had intended. Then she realized what she was saying. "And maybe . . . just maybe . . . I was a little insecure. So, maybe when I thought you didn't like me I started being mean to you so I'd be the one doing the rejecting."

Barbie was so moved by Raquelle's speech. "Raquelle—"

"Remember, I said 'maybe,'" Raquelle added.

Barbie couldn't help but smile. "Got it. Then maybe I should have tried harder to be your friend. I really wanted to. When you first came to school, I was dying to get to know you."

"You're kidding," said Raquelle.

"We were in acting class, and you seemed

so confident and talented. I thought it would be great to be your friend. But then you were so distant, and mean. I figured you just didn't like me." She paused for a moment. "I definitely should have tried harder. You were the one in a new place. I should have been the one to reach out. I'm sorry I never invited you to sit with me at lunch. I should have."

"Thanks. And I'm sorry I glared at you and turned away so much," Raquelle apologized. "Can you forgive me? Do you think we can be friends?"

Barbie smiled again. "I think we are friends," she said as she hugged Raquelle.

Suddenly, they heard Carrie gasp. "Look!" she cried. The FurySphere was glowing until the bars turned into dancing, sparkling lights. Sparkles were swirling around Barbie and Raquelle. Then the bars disappeared completely. Barbie looked at Raquelle. Her clip-on wings had also vanished, but in their place were huge, incredible, beautiful real wings!

"Barbie! Raquelle! The cage! Your wings!" cried Taylor. Barbie looked at her own wings and saw hers were real, too!

"The cage! The cage is gone!" Barbie cheered with excitement. "But I don't understand, what happened?"

"I don't know," Carrie admitted. "The FurySphere's made of anger. It's supposed to be stronger than anything. . . ."

"Except stronger emotions!" Taylor explained. "Your forgiveness is stronger than Princess Graciella's anger. It transformed the prison of a FurySphere to the freedom of wings—real wings."

"Real wings?" asked Barbie.

"I guess forgiveness lets you fly!" Carrie added.

Barbie gasped. "Raquelle! Now we can get to the wedding!"

"Yes!" said Raquelle as they hurried to leave. As she and Barbie flew out of the room toward a passageway, Carrie and Taylor cried out to them, "Hurry! Good luck!" Barbie knew she'd need it.

Chapter 9

The wedding hall was filled with the citizens of Gloss Angeles. After all, this was the biggest marriage of the century.

Zane and Crystal were sitting in the audience. "Think of it this way, Zane. Soon it will all be over and you'll be free to heal your heart with someone else," she said soothingly. She held up her necklace and snapped a picture of her and Zane together. Zane barely noticed. He was too concentrated on Princess Graciella.

Ken was standing at the altar. He was

held in place by swirls of magical sparkles. He struggled to break free from them but without success. Ken could see the first bridesmaid flying down the aisle. He was running out of time!

A few moments later, Princess Graciella flew down the aisle. Even though she looked pretty, all Ken could think about was Barbie. Princess Graciella stood beside him.

"Do you, Ken, take Princess Graciella to be your lawfully wedded fairy wife?" the male fairy conducting the ceremony asked. Ken tried his best to keep his mouth closed, but Princess Graciella sent a burst of sparkles from her hand and made him blurt, "Mmmmphf . . . I do."

The fairy conducting the wedding continued, "Then, by the power vested in me, I now pronounce you—"

"I object!" Zane yelled.

"You already objected!" shouted the princess. "You can't object again!"

"I can, and I will!" cried Zane. "You're making a terrible mistake," he said as he flew over to her and got down on one knee. "Listen to your true heart, Princess Graciella. If you are under a love potion, fight it. Please, let the human go and marry me," he begged.

Ken could not agree more. But the princess was more annoyed than wooed. She turned to the fairy in charge of marrying her and Ken.

"Please continue," she said with irritation in her voice.

"I now pronounce you husband and—"

"Wait!" Barbie shouted.

Everyone in the crowd turned and

gasped as they saw Barbie and Raquelle flying in with their beautiful new wings. No one was more excited to see them than Ken.

"Raquelle? Barbie!" he cried.

"We object to this wedding!" shouted Barbie.

Princess Graciella was beyond annoyed now. "What, again? Can't a girl get a husband around here?"

"We object on the grounds that the

princess is acting under the influence of a love potion," Raquelle said.

"I've had enough of this nonsense!" exclaimed Princess Graciella as she shot magical sparkles at Barbie and Raquelle. But with their new wings, Barbie and Raquelle were extra quick. They dodged the sparkles with ease. Princess Graciella was not ready to give up. "Someone get them, now!" she ordered. Her attendants flew after Barbie and Raquelle.

Barbie knew she needed to act quickly. "Cover me. I'm going to try to get to Princess Graciella with the antidote," she said to Raquelle.

Raquelle nodded in agreement. "Hey, everybody, check out the new wings. They're huge! I dare you not to catch a target this big!" she taunted. Princess Graciella was so furious that she hurled sparkles right at Raquelle. While the princess had her focus on Raquelle, Barbie flew over Princess Graciella, took out the mist, and released it right above her.

The beautiful mist sparkled all around the princess. The crowd watched as her eyes changed from purple back to clear blue.

Crystal knew exactly what was going on. She had to get out of there and fast! "I think I hear my mom calling. Gotta fly!"

But Ken wasn't going to let the person who got them into this mess in the first place get away.

"Uh-uh. Not so fast," he said as he caught up to her.

Soon the sparkles around Princess Graciella disappeared. "What? Where? A wedding dress? I . . . I remember everything!" Princess Graciella said as she began to realize where she was and why she was wearing a wedding dress. "Crystal! You did give me a love potion, didn't you? We were going through your fashion pictures, and you gave me a drink, and that's when I saw . . . Oh, Kip, I am so, so sorry. . . ." she said.

"Um, it's Ken, actually. But it's okay. I understand you weren't really yourself," Ken replied.

"No, I wasn't," said Princess Graciella, turning to Crystal. "How could you?" she cried.

"All I wanted was a chance with Zane! Not that it helped. He loves you no matter what," Crystal tried to explain.

"I do," said Zane. "Thank you for bringing her back to me," he said to Barbie and Raquelle.

"Yes, thank you," Princess Graciella added. "Please, let me do something for you in return."

Barbie and Raquelle looked at each other. "Release Carrie and Taylor from the dungeons and lift their banishment," Barbie requested.

"But they betrayed me," Princess Graciella protested. "The three of us were friends, then they became so close, they cut me out."

"They don't remember it that way at all," explained Barbie.

"They don't?" asked Princess Graciella. She decided she would get an answer straight from Carrie and Taylor. With a wave of her hand and a shot of sparkles, Carrie and Taylor appeared before everyone.

"That was fun!" Carrie giggled.

"Carrie and Taylor, did you or did you not become best friends, then betray me by dropping me entirely?" Princess Graciella asked.

"No," said Taylor. "We only spent time without you because you got so busy with royal duties. You were never free."

"But you stopped inviting me to do things," replied Princess Graciella.

"We were sure you'd say no, so we didn't try," explained Taylor. She thought for a moment. "That was a mistake," she admitted.

Carrie nodded in agreement. "We're sorry. Can you forgive us?" she asked.

"If you can forgive me for reacting so badly instead of just talking to you and learning the truth," Princess Graciella said as she hugged Carrie and Taylor.

"You know," Crystal interrupted, "as long as there's all this forgiveness going around..."

"I'll forgive you, Crystal, but only after you pay for what you have done. I think doing every single bit of cleaning after the wedding reception would be a fine punishment, don't you?" the princess said.

Ken was suddenly worried. "Um, did you say 'wedding reception'?"

"Yes," Princess Graciella said . . . only this time she was saying it to Zane. "I seem to remember you on one knee asking me to marry you."

"Is this a yes?" Zane beamed.

"Yes!" replied Princess Graciella. Zane picked Princess Graciella up and swung her around in his arms. Everyone in the room clapped . . . even Crystal. The two stepped up to the altar and shared their wedding vows. Barbie, Raquelle, and Ken were sitting in the front row. Taylor and Carrie were bridesmaids.

As the happy couple left the building, everyone grabbed a handful of magical sparkles out of Carrie's purse and tossed them in the air.

Barbie and Raquelle smiled at each other. They could not believe the day they had, and especially that they shared it together!

"I've seen a lot of incredible things today, but nothing as weird as you guys acting like friends," said Ken.

"Pretty cool, right?" Barbie replied.

"Very cool," Raquelle answered.

Princess Graciella smiled at the group of amazing friends in front of her. "Thank you all for helping me. It's been a true pleasure getting to know you." She waved her hand, sending a beautiful swirl of sparkles that grew and wrapped around Barbie, Raquelle, and Ken.

The next morning, Barbie woke up in her bed, confused. She got dressed and went to meet Ken at Wally's Diner. But she couldn't help thinking about the dream she'd had the night before. It had just seemed so *real*.

When Barbie arrived at Wally's, Ken was waiting. He'd had a weird dream, too! Neither of them could remember the details exactly, but some of what they did remember was hard to believe.

"It's weird . . . but the *really* weird thing is I have this incredibly strong feeling that in the dream, Raquelle and I . . . we were *friends*," Barbie said.

Ken couldn't believe it. "Friends?"

"I know, like she'd ever let that happen!"

Just then, Raquelle walked into the diner and flashed Barbie a huge smile. "Supercute outfit! Where did you get it? Mind if I join you?" Raquelle asked.

Barbie was too amazed to speak.

"What?" Raquelle asked.

Barbie smiled. "You're being really nice to me. Believe me, I like it, it's just different."

"I don't really get it either," Raquelle said. "I had this dream last night, and I can't remember the details, but I woke up feeling like we're friends. Good friends."

Barbie and Ken exchanged a look, just as Carrie and Taylor came in, too. They were looking for Barbie . . . and Raquelle.

"We wanted to stop in and say good-bye," Taylor said.

"Good-bye?" Barbie asked.

"We've reconnected with an old friend," Carrie explained. "So we're going to spend some time in our hometown."

"It was great hanging out with you both, though. We know we'll see you again," Taylor added.

Raquelle was confused. "Hanging out with you? But I barely even know you."

Carrie and Taylor looked suddenly

embarrassed. "Oooh, look at the time! Gotta fly!" Taylor said, tugging Carrie toward the door.

"Bye!" Barbie called after them, confused, but happy for her friends.

Raquelle smirked. "Looks like your stylists skipped town. Guess we know one star who won't shine as brightly on the next red carpet, hmm?"

Barbie raised her eyebrows. *What happened to the new, friendly Raquelle?*

"Oopsie. Guess old habits die hard, girl," Raquelle said, giving Barbie a gentle nudge.

Raquelle broke into a grin as Ken and Barbie laughed. They kept talking over french fries and milk shakes. They might not ever figure out what happened the night before, but one thing was for sure—this could be the start of a new friendship!